INDY
and MR. LINCOLN

Written by Natalia M. Belting
Illustrated by Leonard Everett Fisher

Henry Holt and Company New York

In Canada, George J. McLeod, Ltd.

Library of Congress Catalog Card Number: 60-6598

90890-0210

Printed in the United States of America

Indy and Mr. Lincoln

TODAY SOMETHING HAD TO HAPPEN, Indy thought, something has to happen today. Not a thing had happened for days. Not a thing had happened except the rain. It had rained and rained and rained. Day after day it had rained.

Indy was tired of the rain.

Indy stood at the door of the Allen's log cabin. The spring sun was shining. Today, Indy said to herself, there is no rain. Today something is going to happen. Something besides rain is going to happen.

Indy was a pig. She was a small white pig. She was as round as this. She was not a bit bigger than that. There was not another pig in New Salem like Indy.

The other pigs in New Salem had to live outdoors. They

had to sleep in piles of leaves under the trees. They had to find their own food.

Indy lived inside. She lived in a log cabin with Dr. Allen and Mrs. Allen and Molly Allen. All the people in New Salem lived in log cabins. All the pigs in New Salem lived outside. All the pigs except Indy lived outside. She lived inside with people.

Her name was not Indy. Her name was Indiana because she had been born in Indiana. It was just that she was called Indy for short. There was no pig in New Salem with such a fine name. There was no other pig in New Salem with a name at all.

There was no other white pig. Indy was white as the snow that fell in the winter. She was so white that the sun burned her skin in the summer. The sun turned her skin pink and then red.

"This will not do at all," Mrs. Allen said. So she made a

calico jacket and a pair of small trousers for Indy. She made a sunbonnet that tied under Indy's chin.

Then Indy could go out in the sun in the summer. Indy liked the jacket and the trousers and the bonnet. The girls and the boys in New Salem laughed when they saw Indy. Dr. Allen laughed. Mrs. Allen laughed. Molly laughed.

Everybody laughed at Indy when she wore her jacket and her trousers and her bonnet. Mr. and Mrs. Rutledge who kept

the inn on the top of the hill laughed. Ann Rutledge laughed.

Denton Offut laughed. "Re-mark-able!" Mr. Offut said. "Re-mark-able! A most re-MARK-able pig," he said and he laughed.

Mr. Lincoln who kept the store with Mr. Offut laughed.

Everybody in New Salem laughed at Indy. There was not another pig in New Salem like Indy. Mr. Offut said it. Indy was a re-MARK-able pig. And she knew it.

Indy stood in the door and looked up the street. She looked down the street. The other pigs in New Salem were out in the street. They were walking in the mud. They were rolling in the mud.

I am not like those pigs, Indy said to herself. I am a clean pig. And she was. Indy was a very clean pig. Indy took a bath in a round wood tub. On Saturdays Molly put Indy in the tub and washed her. Molly washed her ears and scrubbed her back. Indy was as clean a pig as ever there was. Indy was not at all like the other pigs in New Salem.

"Indy," Mrs. Allen said.

Indy looked. Molly was cleaning the kettles that hung in the fireplace. Mrs. Allen was sweeping the floor. Mrs. Allen said, "You are in the way, Indy. We are cleaning house today. You will have to go outside."

Indy looked at Mrs. Allen. "Indiana," Mrs. Allen said,

"you heard me. Go outside. The sun is not too hot. You do not need your jacket and your trousers and your bonnet. Get out, Indiana!" Mrs. Allen said again. "You are in the way."

Indy stepped out into the sun. She heard Mr. Onstot working in his shop. She went down the street to Mr. Onstot's shop. Mr. Onstot made many things. He made things out of wood. Most of the time what he made were barrels. He made big barrels and middle sized barrels and small barrels that were smaller than the small barrels. He made barrels that were bigger than the big barrels. His shop was full of barrels.

Indy walked in. Mr. Onstot was working at his bench. There was a pile of wood shavings at the end of the bench. Indy liked the smell of the shavings. She buried her nose in them.

"Well, now," Mr. Onstot said, "I seem to have a visitor." Then he laughed. "A visitor! A pig! A most remarkable pig,"

he said. "Good morning, Indy," he said. "I see you have taken to wearing curls," he said, and he laughed.

Indy tossed her head. She tossed off the curls of wood that had caught on her ears.

Mr. Onstot went back to his work. Indy looked at the barrels. There were barrels that were all done. There were barrels that were not done. There was a very small barrel.

Indy put her front feet up on the edge of the small barrel. She looked inside. It was dark. It was hard to see what was in the barrel. She put her head into the barrel. Her front feet slipped. All at once she was in the barrel. She was upside down in the barrel, and she could not get out.

"In-di-ana!" Mr. Onstot scolded. "You always get into something! A barrel now!" He pulled Indy out of the barrel. He set her down on her feet. "Get out, Indiana!" he said. "I have work to do. Get out. Do you hear me, Indiana?"

Indy went out. Today something was going to happen. But it was not going to happen in Mr. Onstot's shop. There were only barrels in his shop. Nothing happened in barrels.

She crossed the street. She was careful about the mud. She was not like the other pigs of New Salem. She did not like to get in the mud.

Mr. Miller lived across the street. Mr. Miller was a black-smith. Mr. Miller was working. Indy could tell. There was smoke coming out of the chimney of his blacksmith shop. There was always work for Mr. Miller. Indy looked at the pots and the kettles by the cabin door. There were all kinds of pots and kettles. Big ones and small ones. New ones that Mr. Miller had made. Old ones that were waiting for Mr. Miller to mend.

Indy looked at the cabin door. Mr. Miller was working at the fire. He was making horseshoes. It was hot in the cabin. Too hot to go in.

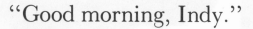

"Good morning, Indy."

Indy looked. Mrs. Miller was out back of the cabin. She had a fire burning under a big kettle. Mrs. Miller was making soap. Indy knew the smell of soap.

Indy looked at Mrs. Miller. Indy knew about soap cooking in a big kettle. Sometimes it boiled over. Sometimes, if you were too close, it boiled over on you. Indy did not want to get in Mrs. Miller's way.

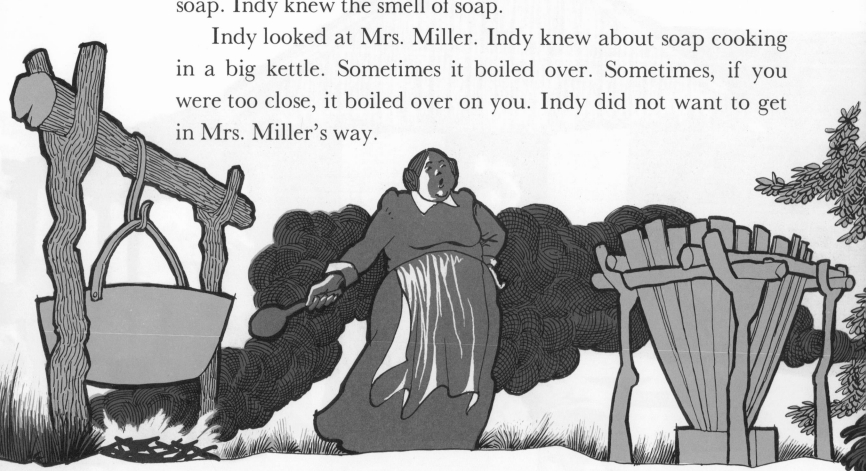

Nothing is going to happen here, Indy said to herself. Mr. Miller is making horseshoes. Mrs. Miller is making soap. Nothing is going to happen here.

Down the street was the cabin where Mr. and Mrs. Hill lived. Mrs. Hill kept geese. Indy remembered the geese. They were silly birds. She would see what the geese were doing.

Silly birds, Indy thought, geese are silly birds, and she started for the Hill's cabin.

"In-di-ana!" Indy heard Mrs. Miller call her. "Watch out, Indiana!"

Indy looked over her shoulder. She did not look to see where she was going. She did not see the vegetable cellar in front of her. She did not see that the door was off the vegetable cellar. She did not see the hole in front of her.

Indy fell in. She fell in on top of the potatoes. She slipped on the onions. She sat down on a pile of carrots. And she could not get up.

"In-di-ana!" Mrs. Miller scolded. "There never was such a pig for getting into trouble," she said. She lifted Indy out of the vegetable cellar. Then she laughed. Mrs. Miller laughed and laughed and laughed.

There was nothing to laugh about. Indy was sure there was not a thing to laugh about. Indy was not laughing. Indy was crying. The tears rolled out of her eyes. She could not help it. The onions made her cry.

Mrs. Miller laughed. "Get along, Indiana! One way or

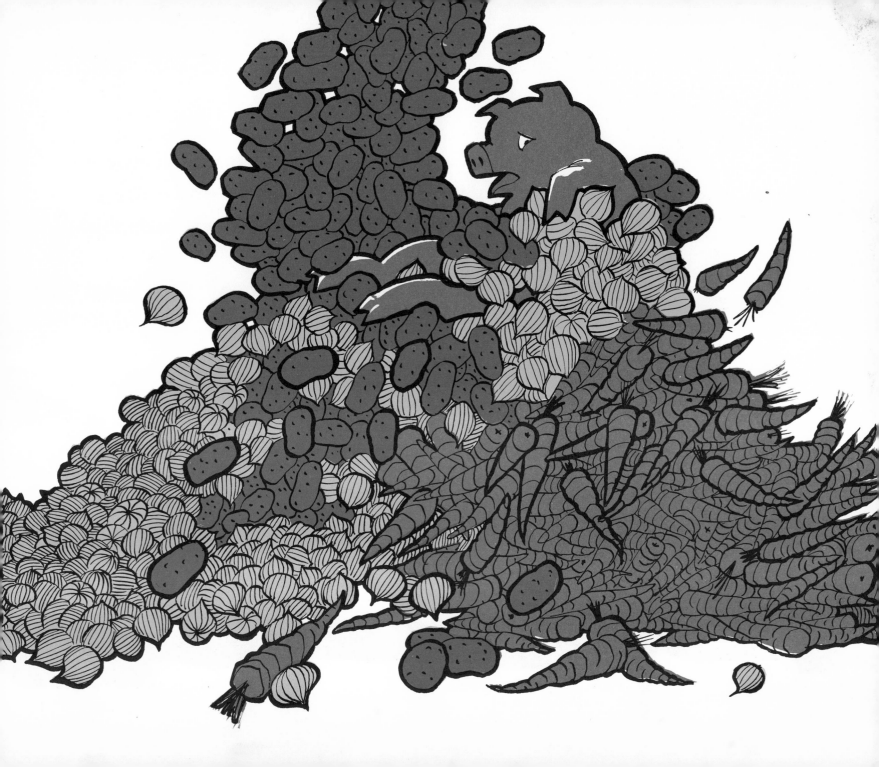

another, I will not get a thing done, for getting you out of trouble or for laughing at you. Get along. I have work to do."

By the time she came to the Hill's cabin Indy had stopped crying. She looked for the geese. There they were. They were on the other side of the cabin. She would have some fun. They were silly birds. She could scare them.

Indy went around to the other side of the cabin. She went carefully so the geese did not hear her. Indy ran at the geese.

Indy chased the geese. She chased them around the cabin. It was fun. They looked so silly when they ran. They stretched out their wings. They stretched out their necks and they ran.

Indy chased them around the cabin again. She stopped to catch her breath. Something bit her hind leg. She had forgotten the gander. She had forgotten all about the gander when she was chasing the geese. The gander was bigger than any of the geese. The gander was not afraid of anybody. Indy knew. The gander was not afraid of Mr. Hill or Dr. Allen or

Mr. Offut or Mr. Onstot. The gander was not afraid of Indy.

Indy was afraid of the gander.

Indy ran. She ran as fast as she could. The gander had a long beak. He had a long neck. He was right behind Indy. He stretched his neck. He bit Indy again. She could not run fast enough to get away from him.

Indy ran across the street. She ran through the mud. It didn't matter. She had to get away from the gander. She ran

as fast as she could run. She ran straight across the open yard in front of the Rutledge's inn.

Ann was out in the yard. Ann was spreading the wash on the grass to dry in the sun.

The gander was at Indy's heels. He was going to bite her again.

"In-di-ana!" Ann said. "In-di-ana!"

Indy knew. She had run across the clean clothes. She had

run across the sheets and tablecloths. She had run across them with her muddy feet.

But the gander was chasing her. She had to run. The gander was right behind her. He was chasing her straight into the rail fence.

Indy ran up hard against the fence. She hit the fence with her head. One of the rails fell off on the ground.

Indy was a small pig. She was a very small pig. She went

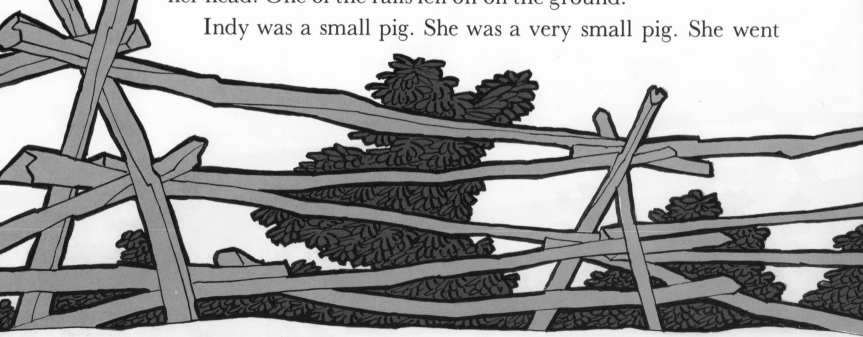

through the fence. She went through the place where the rail had fallen off.

The gander bit her. He bit her twice. But she got through the fence.

And the gander could not get through. The gander had a yoke on his neck. Mr. Hill had put the yoke on the gander's neck so that he could not get through a rail fence.

Indy sat down. She was safe from the gander. She was on

this side of the fence. The gander was on that side of the fence.

Indy was on this side of the fence. She was in the middle of the berry bushes. It was too early for berries. It was not too early for the thorns. Indy stood up. She stood up all at once. The thorns scratched. They were as bad as the gander biting her. They scratched her wherever they touched her.

Indy looked through the hole in the fence. The gander was waiting for her. She could not go back through the fence. She walked through the bushes. The thorns scratched. She wished she had not gone through the fence. The gander would not have bitten her any worse.

She came to the edge of the bushes. She came to the edge of the road. The road was muddy from all the rain. The mud looked soft. The mud looked cool.

Indy walked into the mud. She sat down slowly in the mud. The mud felt good. The mud took the sting out of the scratches.

The mud covered over the places the gander had bitten.

Indy shut her eyes and sat still in the soft, wet, cool mud.

The gander has gone back, Indy thought after awhile. If I am careful he will not see me. It is time I went back home.

Indy tried to stand up. She could not. She tried to get her feet back under her. The mud held them tight.

The harder she tried to stand up, the more the mud pulled. Every time, the mud pulled her back.

The mud pulled her down. She was in the mud up to her middle. She was in the mud up to her ears. It was almost up to her snout. The mud was burying her. The mud was burying her and nobody would ever know what had become of her.

"In-di-ana!"

It was Mr. Lincoln. "In-di-ana!" he said and laughed. "The things that happen to you!" He looked down at Indy. He was a very tall man. He had to look a long way down at

Indy. "There you are in the mud. Here I am on my way to Springfield. Here I am in my Sunday clothes, all dressed up for the city folks. And there you are stuck in the mud."

It didn't matter, Indy thought. Nothing mattered. This was the last thing that was going to happen to her. The mud was going to bury her.

"Don't worry," Mr. Lincoln said. Don't worry, Indiana,"

Mr. Lincoln said, "I'll get you out. I can go to Springfield another day."

Mr. Lincoln took a rail off of the fence. "This ought to do it," he said. He pushed the rail into the mud under Indy. He pushed hard on the rail. He was bent double, pushing down on the rail.

Indy felt the rail under her. She felt the rail lift her.

Sqr...k, sqlu...sh, sqr...k went the mud. The rail lifted Indy out of the mud.

Ker...plop! Indy landed on the grass by the edge of the road.

Mr. Lincoln was down flat. Half of him was in the mud. Half of him was on the grass. Mr. Lincoln sat up. Mr. Lincoln looked at Indy. He looked at his clothes. "I reckon," he said,

and he laughed, "I reckon, Indy, the only way folks will be able to tell us apart is by the length of our legs. Mine are a mite longer than yours," he said and he laughed again.

Indy didn't know. She was just glad Mr. Lincoln had come by when he did. She was covered with mud. She didn't care. She just hoped nothing would ever happen again. Nothing.